The Owl and the Pussy Cat

A FOLK TALE CLASSIC

EDWARD LEAR • PAUL GALDONE

HOUGHTON MIFFLIN HARCOURT
Boston   New York

For information about permission to reproduce selections from
this book, write to Permissions, Houghton Mifflin Harcourt
Publishing Company, 215 Park Avenue South, New York,
New York 10003.
www.hmhco.com

The Library of Congress has cataloged the hardcover edition
as follows: Lear, Edward, 1812–1888. The owl and the pussy-cat.
Summary: After a courtship voyage of a year and a day, Owl and
Pussy finally buy a ring from Piggy and are blissfully married.
1. Children's poetry, English. [1. Nonsense verses. 2. Animals—
Poetry. 3. English poetry.]   I. Galdone, Paul, ill. II. Title.
PR4879.L209 1987b   821'.8   86-17034

ISBN: 978-0-899-19854-5 paperback
ISBN: 978-0-544-39295-3 paper over board

Manufactured in China
SCP 10 9 8 7 6 5 4 3 2 1
4500509232

For Esie, Joanna, and Jamie,
Paul Ferencz and Phoebe

The Owl and the Pussy-cat went to sea

In a beautiful pea-green boat,

They took some honey,
and plenty of money,
Wrapped up in a five-pound note.

The Owl looked up
to the stars above,

And sang to a small guitar,

"O lovely Pussy! O Pussy, my love,
What a beautiful Pussy you are,

You are,
You are!
What a beautiful Pussy you are!"

Pussy said to the Owl,
"You elegant fowl!
How charmingly sweet you sing!

O let us be married! too long we have tarried:

But what shall we do for a ring?"

They sailed away,
for a year and a day,
To the land where
the Bong-tree grows

And there in a wood
a Piggy-wig stood,

With a ring at the end of his nose,
His nose,
His nose,
With a ring at the end of his nose.

"Dear Pig, are you willing
to sell for one shilling

Your ring?"
Said the Piggy, "I will."

So they took it away,
and were married next day
By the Turkey who
lives on the hill.

They dined on mince,
and slices of quince,

Which they ate
with a runcible spoon;

And hand in hand,
on the edge of the sand,
They danced by the light of the moon,

The moon, the moon,

They danced by the light of
the moon.